CUENTO DE LUZ

To Jo Beth

- Erik Speyer -

The Adventures of Kubi

Text © Erik Speyer
Illustrations © Erik Speyer
This edition © 2015 Cuento de Luz SL
Calle Claveles, 10 | Urb. Monteclaro | Pozuelo de Alarcón | 28223 | Madrid | Spain
www.cuentodeluz.com

The author is grateful to Hans Kemp for the use of his Vietnam photographs
as a resource for this book.

ISBN: 978-84-16147-35-9

Printed by Shanghai Chenxi Printing Co., Ltd. January 2015, print number 1477-4

FSC
www.fsc.org
MIX
Paper from
responsible sources
FSC® C007923

The Adventures of

Erik Speyer

On a farm in a small village in Vietnam
there lived a little dog named Kubi.

He had many friends on the farm.
He was very happy there.

Every day Kubi said good morning
to his best friend Ang, a large water buffalo,
before Ang left to work in the rice fields.

Kubi also said good morning
to his other friends on the farm.

There was the duck family,
who spent most of the day paddling around near
the flooded rice fields, and the pig family,
who passed most of the day sleeping in the shade,
or rooting in the mud.

Kubi's favorite thing was to ride on Ang's back
as he pulled a plow through the muddy fields.
The rice fields, which were flooded with water,
had to be plowed before rice could be planted.

After school, Kubi would play with the children.
Together they would cross a narrow bridge,
called a monkey bridge.

He was very agile and could easily run across the bridge.

One night,
there was a big
celebration for Tet,
the Vietnamese New Year,
at the farmhouse. It was so noisy that
Kubi couldn't go to sleep. He decided to
find a cozy spot away from the noise,
and he fell asleep on some wooden boards.

But in the dark night he could not tell that
they were part of a boat!

When Kubi woke up the next morning,
he was sitting in the boat among many other boats.
The women in the boats were all waiting
for the large fishing boats to come home.

Once the fishing boats arrived,
the women would load the fish onto their boats
and take them to the market, in a town called Hoi An.

Kubi explored Hoi An
and found an old Japanese bridge
where there was a good view.
He was hoping to see his little village,
but all he could see was water and fishing boats.

He had come to a place where boats were repaired when it started to rain quite hard. Kubi ran around trying to find a dry spot away from the rain.

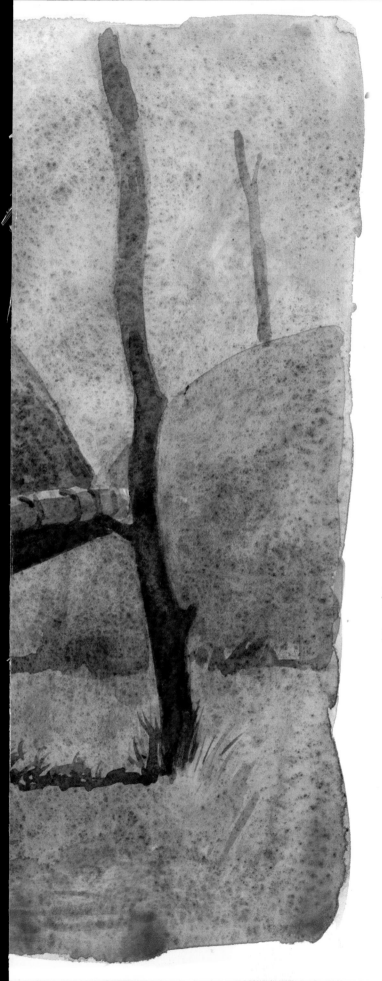

Kubi spent the night under a reed boat.

He was lonely and miserable. At his farm they always fed him in the morning and at night.

Here there was no one to feed him and he was hungry...

In the morning, a lady gave him a ride in her basket boat and he looked to see if he could find his farm. He rode on the boat for a long time, but all he saw was more water and fishing boats.

The next day, Kubi went to the market in Hoi An
to find something to eat. He saw women selling garlic, onions,
dried mushrooms, tomatoes, limes, peppers,
and other things he didn't like.

He was very hungry.

Finally, a lady with a small kitchen gave him some food that he liked.

It was fish soup with noodles and he thought it was the best thing he had ever eaten. She carried the whole kitchen on her shoulders and put it down on the sidewalk every day to sell the soup. She even carried a small coal fire in the basket to keep the soup hot.

At the market he saw a lot of ducks kept inside basket cages. Kubi thought about his duck friends on the farm, so he let these ducks go free by lifting the baskets with his little nose.

Just then a group of boys set off some firecrackers.
The ducks were frightened and started flying
around the marketplace, causing a great panic.

The ladies from the market tried to chase the ducks away
and fruit and vegetables went everywhere.

Kubi had to run from the market ladies since they blamed him for the ducks getting loose and the big mess they had made. Some of the ladies chased him through the streets of Hoi An.

Just then, another dog came running up to Kubi
and showed him how to get away from the angry ladies.

Long, Kubi's new friend, took him behind a temple column where they waited for the ladies to go back to the market.

Long then took Kubi to where he lived,
on board a large fishing boat tied up
next to a lot of other fishing boats.

They had a good time together,
sitting in the shade watching
all the activity in the harbor.

The next day, a friendly cyclo driver from Kubi's town saw him and called him over to give him a ride home.

Kubi was happy to be on his way back home and enjoying his first cyclo ride.

When he got back to the farm, Kubi greeted all his
friends and told them of his adventures.
Kubi was glad to be able to race around with
his friends the little pigs again.

Then he hopped up onto Ang's great back,
his favorite place to sleep. He fell asleep instantly,
happy to be back under the moonlit sky of his home.